THE PRINCESS AND THE PEGASUS

A.M. Luzzader

Illustrated by Anna M. Clark

Published by Knowledge Forest Press
P.O. Box 6331
Logan, UT 84341

Ebook ISBN-13: 978-1-949078-65-7
Paperback ISBN-13: 978-1-949078-64-0

Cover design by Sleepy Fox Studio, www.sleepyfoxstudio.net

Editing by Chadd VanZanten

Interior illustrations by Anna M. Clark, annamclarkart.com

For Juniper, climb to the highest heights!—A.M.L.

For my mother-in-law, Jen, for all the support she has given me in my illustration career. —A.M.C.

The real-life Princess Olivia and Princess Juniper

CONTENTS

CHAPTER ONE

A STRANGE FEELING IN THE AIR

In a faraway place, in a faraway time, there was a land called Wildflower Kingdom.

Wildflower Kingdom was a beautiful place. It was full of grassy meadows, tall trees, and sparkling streams. At the edges of the kingdom, there were rolling hills and snowy mountains.

And, of course, there were wildflowers everywhere! A place called Wildflower Kingdom must have wildflowers. It would be weird if it didn't. In Wildflower Kingdom, wildflowers grew everywhere and at all times of the year. Wildflowers even grew in the winter. Sometimes, the wildflowers were a problem. There were so many wildflowers everywhere, it was hard to pass them by.

Everyone wanted to stop and see them, smell them, and maybe pick a few. Many people in Wildflower Kingdom were late to school and work because of the wildflowers.

There was a village in Wildflower Kingdom, with cobblestone roads and little shops. It was called Wildflower Village. In the middle of the village was a cafe that served hot chocolate. Next door there was a bakery that made fresh bread and delicious muffins. It was said in Wildflower Kingdom that the smells of cocoa and warm bread were so wonderful, it might spoil your appetite!

Just down the street, there was also a bookshop with very tall bookshelves. The bookshelves were so tall, they built a second story on the shop to make them fit. But it still wasn't tall enough, so they built a third story on top of the second. At last the shelves fit inside the bookshop, but then they had to bring in ladders on wheels to reach all the books.

Next door to the bookshop was a flower shop with bouquets of the wildflowers. They were colorful and smelled wonderful.

Across the street from the flower shop there was a hat shop. The hat shop offered hats of every kind and color. There were tall hats and round hats and hats with long feathers. There were hats for working outside, hats for parties, and hats for all occasions. If they didn't have the hat you were looking for, they would make it for you, right on the spot.

On a hill at the center of the kingdom stood Wildflower Castle. It was made of bright white stone and had many towers. On top of the towers were spires. Flying from the spires were colorful flags and banners that waved gently in the breeze.

Wildflower Kingdom was a peaceful place. They had a dragon who lived in a cave in the mountains, who watched for danger and kept everyone safe.

Wildflower Castle was home to the royal staff, which included a chef, party planners, and workers who took care of the unicorns in the unicorn stables.

The castle was also the home of the royal family. There were four people in the royal family. Queen Jennifer was wise and kind. She had green eyes and long, brown hair. King Andrew told the best jokes. He was tall with blue eyes and a thick, black beard. King Andrew and Queen Jennifer had two daughters, Princess Olivia and Princess Juniper.

Princess Olivia was eight years old. She had green eyes like her mother's. Sometimes, Olivia thought she might like to be a queen when she grew up, like her mother. Other days she thought she might be a teacher when she grew up. Olivia also thought she might want to write books someday, like the books she saw at the library and the bookstore. Olivia changed her mind a lot. Sometimes every day, sometimes every hour.

Princess Juniper was the younger sister. She was six years old. Juniper had blue eyes like her father's. She liked to play games, especially tag.

Queen Jennifer

King Andrew

Princess Olivia

Princess Juniper

If you asked Princess Juniper what she'd like to be when she grew up, she might say scientist, circus clown, or unicorn trainer. On other days, she might say she wanted to be a queen or teacher or writer, like Olivia. This is because Princess Juniper really liked Olivia and usually wanted to be just like her.

The two princesses were best friends. Sometimes they argued with each other. Sometimes they had disagreements. Sometimes they teased each other. But even when the two princesses were cross with one another, they were still friends. Together they enjoyed riding unicorns, playing games, and making crowns using the wildflowers.

One day, Princess Olivia and Princess Juniper were outside doing chores. You may think that princesses don't do any chores, but you'd be wrong about that. Princess Olivia and Princess Juniper were responsible for keeping their bedrooms clean. They both had cute bedrooms, but the rooms wouldn't look very princessy if the beds were unmade or there was clothing left on the floor. So, the princesses spent time each day tidying up their bedrooms.

But Wildflower Castle was a big place. Lots of people lived there. It was so large, you could get lost on your way from the living room to the library. Or you might get confused on your way from the dining room to the unicorn stables. And so King Andrew and Princess Jennifer also asked Olivia and Juniper to pitch in to keep the rest of the castle looking nice. They might sweep the long hallways. Or they helped Miss Beets in the kitchen by washing dishes or mopping the floor.

Princess Olivia's favorite chore was watering the beautiful plants that grew in big pots throughout the castle. She loved giving the plants a little drink and seeing how much they had grown since the last time. Olivia's least favorite chore was folding and putting away laundry. She thought it was so boring.

Princess Juniper didn't like any of the chores. She'd much rather go outside and play. Juniper sometimes complained about her chores. Sometimes she tried to avoid them. However, she also knew that the faster she did her chores, the faster they'd be done.

The chore that day was raking the leaves in the castle courtyard. Wildflower Castle had beautiful grounds. There were fountains, walking paths, statues, and of course many flower beds. There were also many, many trees.

The castle's visitors always enjoyed walking through the courtyard because it was a beautiful and peaceful place. The workers who lived in the castle trimmed plants and trees. They planted flowers and watered the grass.

When it was autumn, however, it grew colder and the nights grew longer. This made the tree leaves change colors. The leaves on the maple trees turned orange or red. The aspen leaves turned bright yellow. Then the leaves began to fall to the ground. They fell on the walkways and on the grass and into the fountains.

Some trees at Wildflower Castle, like pine and cedar trees, did not change colors. These trees grew needles instead of leaves, and the needles did not fall to the ground. The pine and cedar trees stayed green all year, and this is why they were called "evergreen trees."

Still, there were so many leaves around Wildflower Castle! Sometimes it seemed as if the castle would be buried in colorful autumn leaves.

And so everyone in the castle worked together to keep the leaves raked up.

Princess Olivia and Princess Juniper were raking up all the leaves that had fallen onto the walking path in the courtyard. If the leaves were left there and became wet from rain or snow, it could become slippery. Or they would block the path.

It was chilly that day in the kingdom. The two princesses wore fuzzy hats with pom-poms on the tops. They wore mittens knitted from bright red wool. They wore warm boots. Their breath turned to mist in the air.

It took a while, but they finally raked all the leaves into one big pile.

But then they jumped into it! This scattered the leaves everywhere.

"Cover me with the leaves!" said Juniper.

"Okay," said Olivia. "Lie down."

Juniper lay down in the grass, and Olivia piled all the leaves on top of Juniper. Olivia could not see Juniper's red wool gloves or the fuzzy pom-pom on Juniper's hat.

"Juniper, are you still under there?" asked Olivia.

Juniper jumped up to her feet and said, "No!"

Now the leaves were scattered again.

"Let's quit playing," said Olivia. She began to rake again. "Let's rake up these silly leaves instead of scattering them. Then we can go inside for some hot apple cider."

"Okay," said Juniper, grabbing her rake, "but not too hot."

"Okay," replied Olivia, "not too hot."

Olivia and Juniper raked and raked. They worked hard. Their cheeks shone like rosy red apples. When they had nearly finished raking the leaves into another big pile, Juniper stopped.

"I feel something strange!" she said. "The hair on the back of my neck is standing up!"

"Me, too!" said Olivia. "I have goosebumps on my arms!"

A strange wind blew. It was different from the cool breeze of autumn. There was excitement in the air. A hum and buzz came from somewhere.

"What does it mean?" said Juniper, searching the sky.

"Let's go and ask Miss Beets," said Olivia.

They hurried to finish raking up the leaves. When they had returned the rakes to the garden shed, they ran to the kitchen to find Miss Beets. The two princesses didn't know it yet, but something strange and interesting was about to occur.

CHAPTER TWO

A SPECIAL VISITOR

Miss Beets was hard at work. She had chores, too. She was planning what to make for supper at Wildflower Castle. Miss Beets was the head chef at the castle. She must plan meals for the royal family as well as all of the staff. There also were visitors to the castle sometimes. They must also be fed.

Miss Beets loved her job. It allowed her to be creative. She prepared the old recipes that everyone liked, such as truffle and wild onion soup. But she tried new recipes, too, such as blueberry tarts with lemon glaze. Sometimes she mixed new recipes with old ones.

Everyone loved Miss Beets' cooking. This made Miss Beets very happy. Everyone in the castle appreciated the hard work she did for Wildflower Kingdom. Queen Jennifer and King Andrew were the leaders of Wildflower Kingdom, but everyone in the castle and in the village had their own jobs to do.

For supper, Miss Beets planned to make yummy squash soup, fresh-baked cornbread, and chocolate cake with raspberry filling. She would also serve a special drink called horchata, which was made with rice and cinnamon. She made a shopping list. She would go to the market to fetch the things she needed to make supper.

Miss Beets finished her shopping list and looked out the window. She saw Princess Juniper and Princess Olivia working in the courtyard. She noticed that their noses and cheeks were rosy.

They are finishing up their chores, thought Miss Beets. *They will probably come here to the kitchen for some hot cider to warm them up.*

Miss Beets knew that the two sisters would be working outside today. She had already warmed up some cider for them. She already had two mugs ready. And she had even baked some hot biscuits for them with soft butter and sweet honey.

Miss Beets watched as the princesses put away their rakes. Then they ran for the kitchen door. She sliced open the biscuits and spread the honey and butter inside. The biscuits were still warm from the oven and the honey and butter melted quickly.

The two princesses came through the kitchen entrance. Miss Beets heard them chattering as they took off their coats and mittens. Next, they hung their outdoor things on some pegs by the kitchen door. At last they rushed into the kitchen.

"Hello, princesses," said Miss Beets.

"Hello, Miss Beets!" cried the princesses.

"Are you ready for something to warm you up?" asked Miss Beets.

"Yes, please!" they replied.

"Then step right this way," said Miss Beets.

"Oh, yummy," said Juniper when she saw the biscuits and cider waiting for them. Juniper rushed to the table and grabbed the biscuit.

"Thank you, Miss Beets!" said Olivia.

Juniper also thanked Miss Beets, but her mouth was already full of biscuit, so it sounded like, "Mank woo, Miss Feets!"

"You're welcome," said Miss Beets, "and thank you for cleaning up the leaves on the walk. That will be lovely when I go to the market."

Olivia and Miss Beets both joined Juniper at the table to eat their biscuits and drink the cider.

Olivia sipped the cider, which was not too hot. She loved the apple and cinnamon flavor. It was the perfect fall drink. She had already forgotten about the strange feeling in the air outside.

But Juniper had not forgotten. "Miss Beets," she said. "Something was strange outside today."

"Oh?" said Miss Beets.

Then Olivia remembered, too. "Oh, yeah," she

said. "There was something odd. The hair on my neck stood up."

"I got goosebumps," added Juniper, holding up her arm and pointing at it.

Miss Beets nodded. "Ah, yes, it is about that time of year. It is time for the flight of the Pegasus."

"The flight of the what?" said Olivia.

"Pegasus," said Miss Beets. "She is a great and magical horse with huge wings. She's a special visitor to Wildflower Kingdom. She flies over the kingdom every year at this time. If you are outside, you can feel something magical in the air. It means the Pegasus will be flying through this area soon."

"Wow!" said Juniper. "A flying horse!"

Both sisters loved the many unicorns that galloped through Wildflower Kingdom. They loved horses, too. But they had never seen a Pegasus. They had never seen a flying horse.

"Will it stop here?" asked Juniper.

"I'm afraid not," said Miss Beets. "The Pegasus will fly very high in the air as she passes over our kingdom. She is flying to her winter home. A lot of birds and animals will also be moving to warmer places as it gets colder here."

"So, we won't even be able to see the Pegasus?" asked Juniper with a frown.

"You can see the Pegasus," said Miss Beets. "But she will be so high in the sky, she will look like a little white speck to you. You will not be able to see her very well from down here on the ground."

Miss Beets and the princesses finished their biscuits and cider. Miss Beets had made the warm snack for them, and so the princesses insisted that she take a rest while they cleaned up after themselves. This was how the princesses showed their appreciation to Miss Beets. Soon they finished washing their mugs and wiping the biscuit crumbs off the table.

Juniper put her hands on her hips. "Listen here, Olivia," she said. "I want to see that Pegasus."

"Okay," said Olivia. "Let's go outside and watch the sky."

"No," said Juniper. "I don't want to see a little white speck. I want to see the flight of the Pegasus up close. I want to see her mane and wings and hooves. I want to say hello to her."

"How?" said Olivia.

"I don't know yet," said Juniper. "Will you help me or not?"

Olivia thought about this. "Sure, maybe," she said.

"You don't sound very excited," said Juniper.

Olivia thought about it. She remembered seeing a Pegasus in a book. She knew it would look a lot like a normal horse or a unicorn, but it would have wings. Then Olivia got an idea.

"Okay," said Olivia. "I will help."

Olivia didn't just want to see the Pegasus. She didn't just want to meet or speak to the Pegasus. Olivia didn't say this to Juniper, but she wanted to ride the Pegasus and fly through the air!

CHAPTER THREE
DIFFERENT PLANS

THE PRINCESSES TOOK their outside clothing from the pegs by the kitchen door. They put on their hats with pom-poms. They slipped on their red wooly gloves. They pulled on their boots. Then they went outside again.

Juniper and Olivia looked up at the pretty blue sky. The sun was shining brightly, and there were only a few clouds. The princesses turned in circles to see the whole sky. They searched in every direction.

"No sign of the Pegasus, yet," said Olivia.

"Good," said Juniper. "We have to figure out how to get up in the sky to see her."

"I know!" said Olivia. "Why don't we just ask Patrick the dragon to give us a ride?"

Juniper shook her head. "That might scare the Pegasus. Not all dragons are friendly like Patrick is. Remember when you were scared of dragons?"

"That's a good point," said Olivia.

The sisters thought about the problem. They didn't know it, but someone was watching them. Someone was hiding behind a tree, watching and listening.

"I've got it!" said Olivia. "We can go to the highest tower of the castle and watch for the Pegasus."

"Okay," said Juniper. "Let's go!"

The two princesses went back inside and took off their outside clothes again. Their hair had gotten very messy from taking off their pom-pom hats.

"I'm getting tired of putting these on and taking them off again," said Olivia, as she kicked off her boots. She thought about leaving her hat and mittens and boots on the floor in the hallway. That would be easier than hanging her things on the pegs by the door. But Olivia knew that if everyone just left their things on the floor, Wildflower Castle would become messy. Everyone must work together to keep the castle looking nice.

And so, even though it would be easier to leave her things on the floor, she hung her hat and mittens on the pegs again. Once again, she put her boots away. Juniper did, too.

Wildflower Castle had an elevator that rose to the highest floors. Olivia and Juniper ran to the elevator and pushed the "up" button. After a while, the elevator came down, and there was a loud "ding!"

When the doors opened, Olivia and Juniper saw Mr. Asher inside. He was the mail clerk of Wildflower Castle. Mr. Asher sorted and delivered the many letters and packages that came to the castle. Both Olivia and Juniper loved it when Asher brought them a surprise letter or package from their grandparents or their aunt, Duchess Melissa.

Mr. Asher stood inside the elevator with a big cart full of letters and packages to deliver that day. He had been visiting the different floors and delivering the mail.

"Is there any mail for me, Mr. Asher?" asked Juniper, standing on her tip-toes to peek inside the cart.

"Not today, Princess Juniper," said Mr. Asher with a smile.

"How about me?" asked Olivia.

"No, Princess Olivia," he answered. "No mail for you, either. Maybe tomorrow!"

"Do you need any help?" asked Juniper.

"No, thank you," said Mr. Asher. "I enjoy going to all the different floors of the castle. I like to deliver the letters and packages. It just takes a long time!"

Juniper was secretly glad that Mr. Asher didn't need their help. She wanted to get to the top of the tall tower to see the Pegasus. But Juniper saw Mr. Asher's cart. It was still very full of packages and letters. The elevator might be busy for quite some time.

Olivia must have had the same thought because she said, "Come on, Juniper, let's take the stairs."

The sisters went to the stairs. They didn't know it, but someone was still watching them. Someone hid around the corner, watching and listening. The princesses did not notice. They went up the stairs, but the watcher followed them.

The stairs of the tall tower circled around in a spiral. At first, the two princesses ran up the stairs two at a time.

"Let's go!" cried Juniper.

After a while they stopped skipping every other step. But they still kept running. The stairs went up and up. Soon they became very tired and climbed the stairs more slowly. It was a long climb.

"How much longer?" said Olivia, wiping sweat from her forehead.

"I don't know," said Juniper, breathing hard. "Let's keep going!"

They climbed very slowly, holding onto the rail. They pulled themselves up as if they were climbing a mountain.

At last they reached the top of the tower.

"Finally!" said Juniper.

They went to the room at the top of the tower.

Inside the room they found a lady named Miss Haven. She was one of the many artists who worked at Wildflower Castle. She painted pictures and created art to decorate the castle.

"Hello, Miss Haven!" said Juniper and Olivia.

"Hello, princesses!" answered Miss Haven.

Miss Haven stood in front of an art easel. She had a paintbrush in her hand. She was working on a new painting. It was to be a painting of the land around the castle. She was looking out the windows of the tall tower and painting the landscape.

In Miss Haven's landscape painting, the girls could already see the forest, the little brook, and of course many, many wildflowers.

"Your painting is lovely!" said Olivia.

"Yes," said Juniper. "I love it!"

"Thank you, princesses," said Miss Haven, cheerfully. "I'm happy to see you. But what are you doing all the way up here?"

"We felt a shift in the air," said Juniper.

"And Miss Beets said it means the Pegasus is coming," said Olivia.

Haven paused and tipped her head.

"Ah, yes," she said. "You're right. Now that you mention it, I can feel it, too. The Pegasus will probably be here soon."

"We want to look out the window so that we can see the Pegasus when she passes by," said Juniper.

"You're welcome to look out the window," said Haven. She moved her easel and painting out of the way. "But I don't think you'll be able to see the Pegasus very well from here. The Pegasus flies very high in the sky. Even higher than this tower. Higher than the mountains, even."

"Oh," said Juniper with a frown.

The two princesses looked out of the window. They did not see the Pegasus. They went back down the stairs.

"How will we ever get to see the Pegasus if it flies so high in the sky?" asked Juniper. "If it's higher than the castle and the mountains, too?"

"We need a new plan," said Olivia. "Let's think about it."

And that's exactly what they did down all 300 steps to the ground floor of the castle. Olivia was worried that they wouldn't think of any ideas because she hadn't thought of any, but then in the last 50 steps, a new idea came to her.

CHAPTER FOUR

BALLOONS!

AFTER GETTING permission from their mom, Princess Olivia and Princess Juniper decided to walk Wildflower Village. They put on their outside things once again and ran out through the courtyard. They were glad that they had cleared all the leaves from the path earlier that day. Then they went down the cobblestone road to the village.

"Okay," said Juniper, "why are we going to the village? And why did I need to bring all my money from the tooth fairy?"

"You'll see," said Olivia.

Both princesses had been saving their tooth fairy money for a long time. Olivia had been saving to buy a new hand mirror. Juniper was saving to buy a new skateboard.

They reached the village. It was nearby. They passed the hot chocolate shop.

"It smells so good!" said Juniper. "I'm cold again. Can we stop and get some hot chocolate?"

"No," said Olivia. "Stick to the plan."

"You haven't told me the plan!" said Juniper.

They passed by the bakery.

"The bakery smells good, too!" said Juniper. "I'm hungry. Can we get a cupcake?"

"No," said Olivia. "Stick to the plan!"

They passed by the bookstore, the flower shop, and the toy store. Finally, Olivia stopped and pointed to someone on the other side of the street.

"That's Wally," said Juniper. "He sells balloons here in the village."

"Yes," said Olivia. "And so?"

"And so what?" said Juniper. "I don't want a balloon today, unless we're going to a parade or the circus."

"Juniper!" snapped Olivia. "We are not going to a circus or a parade."

"Then why do we need balloons?" asked Juniper.

"Sister!" said Olivia. "Think! What do Wally's balloons do?" asked Olivia.

"Well," replied Juniper, scratching her head, "they float."

"Which direction do they float?" asked Olivia.

"Up," said Juniper, shrugging. "Up to the sky."

That is when Juniper understood Olivia's plan.

"Oh!" cried Juniper, placing one hand on her forehead. "The plan is to float up to the sky using Wally's balloons!"

"Yes!" said Olivia. "You finally got it!"

They crossed the street to see Wally.

"Olivia!" said Wally. "Juniper! So nice to see you today. Would you like a balloon?"

"No, thank you," said Olivia.

"No?" said Wally. "You don't want a balloon?"

"No," said Olivia. "We want *all* the balloons!"

"All of them?" asked Wally. "If you girls buy all the balloons, you might float away!"

Juniper looked at Olivia.

"Exactly," Olivia whispered.

The girls counted out their tooth fairy money. The balloons didn't cost much, but they would need to spend all of their saved-up coins.

"Are you sure about this?" asked Juniper.

"It's the Pegasus!" said Olivia. "We have to see it!"

And so they gave Wally all their coins. He gave half of the balloons to Olivia and the other half to Juniper.

So many balloons! They had never held so many at one time. The balloons were of all different colors. They bumped and squeaked against each other.

But Olivia was worried. She was holding half of the balloons, but she wasn't floating up into the air. She wasn't floating even a little bit. Juniper had the other half of the balloons. Juniper was smaller than Olivia, but she wasn't floating, either.

"Let's hurry home, and we can test the balloons," said Juniper. The two princesses ran home with the balloons trailing behind them, but Olivia was still worried.

The strange watcher was behind them. He watched them buy the balloons. Then he smiled and followed them back to the castle.

CHAPTER FIVE

ONE MORE BALLOON

When Juniper and Olivia arrived at the castle, they went inside and found Miss Haven. She helped the princesses tie the balloons to the stair railing so that the balloons wouldn't float away, and then she gave Juniper and Olivia a giant sheet of heavy paper to make a large sign. They used their best markers and paints to make a sign that read:

DEAR PEGASUS! WE WOULD LIKE TO MEET YOU. PLEASE FLY OVER HERE.

"When we fly up in the sky with the balloons," said Juniper, "the Pegasus will see it and come say hi to us."

"Good idea," said Olivia. They decorated the poster with hearts and stars.

Then, they fetched their balloon bundles and went back outside. There in the courtyard, they felt a gentle breeze. It stirred the leaves on the trees and swirled the leaves around on the ground.

"We're going to have to rake the leaves again, soon," said Olivia. Her balloons bonked and bumped in the air above her.

"Not today," said Juniper, tightly holding onto the strings of her balloons. "Today, we're going to fly up to see the flight of the Pegasus!"

39

"I'm not sure," said Olivia. She looked up. "Look at all these balloons. They're not lifting me up into the air."

"Hey, you're right," said Juniper. "I am smaller than you, and the balloons are not floating me into the air, either."

"What should we do?" said Olivia.

"We must run fast across the grass," said Juniper. "If we run fast enough, the balloons will lift us into the air!"

"Of course," said Olivia. "We must run!"

They held their balloons and ran across the grass. They ran as fast as they could. The wind made the balloons wiggle and bounce. But Juniper and Olivia did not fly up into the air. After a while they got tired and stopped.

"I know!" cried Juniper. "We must jump high into the air! Then the balloons will carry us into the sky!"

"Of course," said Olivia. "We must jump!"

They jumped as high as they could. They jumped higher than they'd ever jumped. The balloons did not lift them into the sky.

"I'm jumping as high as I can!" cried Juniper. "Nothing is happening!"

They got tired again and stopped.

"Juniper, give me your balloons," said Olivia.

"But what if you fly away?" said Juniper. "You will see the Pegasus and I won't!"

"We have to try," said Olivia.

Juniper gave her half of the balloons to Olivia.

But nothing happened. Olivia did not float up into the sky.

"Now you give me all of the balloons and let me try," said Juniper.

"But what if you fly away?" said Olivia. "You will see the Pegasus and I won't!"

"We have to try," said Juniper.

Olivia gave all the balloons to Juniper.

But nothing happened again. Juniper did not float up into the air.

Olivia noticed someone standing behind a nearby tree. The person was standing behind the tree and watching them.

"Hey," called Olivia. "Who is that? Who is that standing behind the tree? Have you been following us and watching us?"

A man stepped out from behind the tree. It was their dad, King Andrew!

"It's only me," said King Andrew. "I have been watching you make plans to see the flight of the Pegasus."

"Dad!" shouted the princesses. They ran to him, and they each gave him a big hug.

"I want to see the Pegasus," said Juniper.

"Me, too!" said Olivia.

"I know, I know," said King Andrew. "You have been working so hard on your plans. I'm very proud of you for thinking so creatively."

"Dad," said Olivia, "our plans aren't working. We can't get up into the sky to see the flight of the Pegasus."

"I have a plan you can try," said King Andrew.

"What is it?" cried the two princesses. "Tell us!"

"We can use a balloon," said King Andrew.

"No, Dad," said Juniper. "We tried balloons. They didn't work."

"Yeah, Dad," said Olivia. "The balloon plan was a flop."

"No, my dears," said Andrew. "I am talking about a different kind of balloon. Please follow me."

They followed their father. He walked around the side of the castle. He led them to the backyard of the castle. As they turned the corner, the princesses saw a giant hot-air balloon.

"This is the balloon I was talking about," said King Andrew. "Not a toy balloon. A hot-air balloon! With this balloon, we can fly high enough to see the flight of the Pegasus."

"Hooray!" cried the princesses.

"Miss Beets told me that you wanted to see the Pegasus," said King Andrew. "And so I spoke to Mr. Paris. He is a balloon pilot from the village. He said he would fly us up to the Pegasus."

"Oh, thank you, Dad!" said Juniper.

"Thank you, Dad!" shouted Olivia.

Both of the sisters were very excited. They followed King Andrew to the hot-air balloon. It was made of colorful silk. Under it there hung a basket that people could ride in. The great balloon rose high into the air, almost as high as the tall tower.

Just then, Juniper saw something high in the sky. It was a little white speck. It was moving across the blue sky. Juniper squinted her eyes. It was the Pegasus! She was far away, but Juniper saw her great wings beating in the sky.

"Look!" said Juniper. "It's the flight of the Pegasus!"

CHAPTER SIX

THE FLIGHT OF THE PEGASUS

Mr. Paris's hot-air balloon was a marvelous device. It was made of silk with an opening in the bottom. Inside it was a torch that made a big flame. The flame made the air inside the balloon very hot. The hot air lifted the balloon into the sky. The hot air is what made it fly. Underneath the balloon was basket for passengers.

Juniper, Olivia, and King Andrew walked over to the balloon.

"What shall we do with all these balloons?" asked Juniper, looking at the balloons in her hand.

"We will give them to our friends when we get back," said Olivia.

"That's a great idea," said King Andrew. "That's very nice of you."

The princesses found some big rocks to put on the strings of the balloons to keep them from floating away while they were on the hot-air balloon. Then, Mr. Paris opened a little door in the balloon's basket, and they all stepped inside.

"Welcome aboard, Miss Juniper," said Mr. Paris. "Welcome aboard, Miss Olivia."

"Can you really fly us up to the Pegasus?" asked Olivia.

"Yes," said Mr. Paris. "We can go very high indeed."

"Thank you for letting us ride in your balloon," said Juniper.

Mr. Paris said, "I heard that you girls have been trying to get up into the sky all day. I heard you have tried many plans."

"That's right," said King Andrew. "First, they thought our friend Patrick the dragon might be able to fly them up to the Pegasus. But they didn't want to frighten the Pegasus. They went to the tall tower of Wildflower Castle. But even that wasn't high enough. Finally, they tried toy balloons, but there weren't enough of them."

"They are very clever princesses!" said Mr. Paris.

The hot-air balloon went higher and higher. Soon even Wildflower Castle and Wildflower Village looked tiny. They were very high. There were clouds all around, and a strong wind blew.

"There!" cried Mr. Paris, pointing. "There is the Pegasus!"

They all turned to look. There she was, the Pegasus. She was a large horse with great white wings. She flew through the air. Her tail and mane were long and flowing in the wind.

"Pegasus!" shouted Juniper. "Come over here! We would like to meet you!"

"This way!" yelled Olivia. "Come over this way!"

Juniper and Olivia were very pleased to see the Pegasus. She was beautiful and amazing as she flew on her great wings. But the Pegasus did not seem to hear Juniper or Olivia. Maybe they were too far away. Or maybe the Pegasus was not paying attention. She flew past the hot-air balloon without stopping.

"I'm sorry, princesses," said Mr. Paris. "The Pegasus must be in a hurry to reach her winter home."

"The sign!" said Juniper. "We must show her the sign we made!"

"Yes," said Olivia. "Get the sign!"

The Pegasus was flying away. Mr. Paris and King Andrew helped the girls unroll their sign. It fluttered in the breeze.

Suddenly, the Pegasus turned. At first, she turned only a little. Then she turned toward the hot-air balloon.

"She saw the sign," shouted Olivia. "She's coming this way!"

Soon the Pegasus flew to the balloon. She came right to the basket and nodded her head to Juniper and Olivia.

"Hello, Pegasus!" said Olivia.

"It's nice to meet you!" said Juniper.

The Pegasus nodded her head again. Then she motioned with her nose as if she wanted the girls to get on her back.

"I think she wants to give you a ride on her back!" said King Andrew.

"Oh, Dad," said Olivia. "Can we? Is it okay?"

"Yes," said King Andrew. "But be careful and hold on tight! Pegasus! Do not drop them! It's a long way down!"

The Pegasus nodded, and everyone knew it would be all right.

King Andrew and Mr. Paris helped the princesses get on the Pegasus's back. The girls held on tight. Then the Pegasus flew in circles around the hot-air balloon. Olivia and Juniper shouted with joy. The Pegasus flew high in the sky. Then she flew down to Wildflower Castle just when Queen Jennifer and Miss Beets were returning from the market. They saw Olivia and Juniper riding on the Pegasus.

"They got their wish!" cried Miss Beets.

"It's amazing!" said Queen Jennifer.

They all waved to each other as the Pegasus flew back to the balloon. It was time to end the ride. It was time for the Pegasus to fly to her winter home. The girls carefully got back into the hot-air balloon.

"Oh, thank you, Pegasus!" said Juniper.

"Thank you!" said Olivia. "It was so nice to meet you!"

The Pegasus whinnied in a friendly, happy way. They all patted the Pegasus on her neck.

King Andrew said, "Pegasus, if you are ever flying over our kingdom, and you need fresh green grass to eat, or refreshing water to drink, please visit us. You are always welcome in Wildflower Kingdom!"

The Pegasus whinnied again. She bowed to Juniper, Olivia, King Andrew, and Mr. Paris. Then she spread her mighty wings, turned into the wind, and flew away toward her winter home.

COULD YOU DO ME A FAVOR?

Thank you for reading *The Princess and the Pegasus*. I hope you enjoyed it!

Could you do me a small favor? Would you leave a review of this book with the retailer where it was purchased? Reviews help me to reach new readers. I would really appreciate it!

—A.M. Luzzader

WWW.AMLUZZADER.COM

- blog
- freebies
- newsletter
- contact info

ABOUT THE AUTHOR

A.M. Luzzader is an award-winning children's book author who writes chapter books and middle grade books. She specializes in writing books for preteens including *A Mermaid in Middle Grade and Arthur Blackwood's Scary Stories for Kids who Like Scary Stories*

A.M. decided she wanted to write fun stories for

kids when she was still a kid herself. By the time she was in fourth grade, she was already writing short stories. In fifth grade, she bought a typewriter at a garage sale to put her words into print, and in sixth grade she added illustrations.

Now that she has decided what she wants to be when she grows up, A.M. writes books for kids full time. She was selected as the Writer of the Year in 2019-2020 by the League of Utah Writers.

A.M. is the mother of a 12-year-old and a 15-year-old who often inspire her stories. She lives with her husband and children in northern Utah. She is a devout cat person and avid reader.

A.M. Luzzader's books are appropriate for ages 5-12. Her chapter books are intended for kindergarten to third grade, and her middle grade books are for third grade through sixth grade. Find out more about A.M., sign up to receive her newsletter, and get special offers at her website: www.amluzzader.com.

facebook.com/a.m.luzzader

instagram.com/amluzzader

ABOUT THE ILLUSTRATOR

Anna M. Clark is an artist who loves to draw, tell stories, and buy journals. She has worked as a baker, a math tutor, a security guard, an art teacher, and works now as an illustrator and artist!

She has traveled through Southeast Asia, was born on Halloween (the best holiday ever), and loves to create large chalk art murals. Anna lives with her husband in their cute apartment in Logan, Utah, with their beautiful basil plant.

Explore more of Anna M. Clark's work and her current projects at her website: annamclarkart.com.

OTHER BOOKS BY
A.M. Luzzader

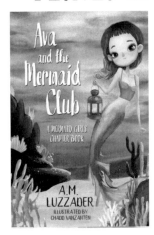 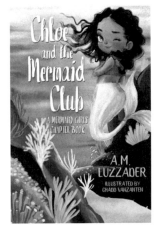

Mermaid Club: A Mermaid Girls Chapter Book

For ages
6-10

 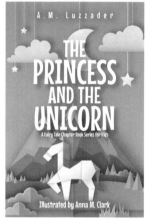
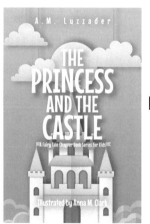

OTHER BOOKS BY
A.M. Luzzader

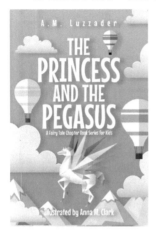 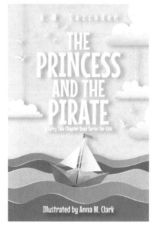

A Fairy Tale Chapter Book Series for Kids

For ages
6-10

OTHER BOOKS BY
A.M. Luzzader

A Magic School for Girls
Chapter Book

For ages
6-8

OTHER BOOKS BY
A.M. Luzzader

Pet Magic

For ages
6-10

OTHER BOOKS BY
A.M. Luzzader

Decker's Video Game Rescue Agency

For ages 6-10

OTHER BOOKS BY
A.M. Luzzader

Small Flames

For ages
6-10